SUE PURKISS
Spook School

First published 2003 by
A & C Black Publishers Ltd
37 Soho Square, London, W1D 3QZ

www.acblack.com

ISBN 0-7136-6292-1

A CIP catalogue for this book is available from the British Library.

Printed and bound in Spain by G. Z. Printek, Bilbao.

SUE PURKISS
Spook School

Illustrated by
Lynne Chapman

A & C Black • London

For Viv, who has been
so generous with her advice
and encouragement.

Chapter One

'In all my years of teaching, alive and dead, I have never, *never*, come across a result like this. One ghost in this class has scored *nought* in every single exam – I repeat, in every single exam. And that ghost is—'

'Nooooooo!' shrieked Spooker Batt, sitting bolt upright in bed.

His mother appeared beside him. 'Goodness, dear, what is it? Did you have a bad dream?'

'The worst,' groaned Spooker. 'I dreamed that I failed every one of my exams, and Sir Rupert was having a go at me in front of the whole class – it was horrible, Mum, horrible! He did that thing with his eyeballs, where he gets crosser and crosser, and they stick out more and more, and then they pop out and roll down his face, and—'

'Yes, yes,' said Mrs Batt hastily, 'I do remember that.' She too had sat and trembled in Sir Rupert Grimsdyke's classes, and she remembered all his little habits only too well; they weren't the kind of thing you easily forgot. Sir Rupert had taught at the Anne Boleyn

Secondary School for hundreds of years, so he'd had plenty of time to perfect the art of making his students' lives a misery.

'You mustn't worry about the exams,' Mrs Batt said. 'Dreams don't always come true. You've been doing fine in – well, most of your subjects.'

'Yes,' said Spooker miserably, 'but not in Practical Haunting. Sir Rupert really doesn't like me. He shouts, and then I get all muddled up, and then I make a mess of things, and then he gets even crosser, and then—'

'Sir Rupert doesn't like anyone,' said his mother briskly. 'Never did. It's not in his nature to like people. But there's no point worrying about it. You'll just have to put up with it, like everyone else does. Come on, it's getting dark – you might as well get up and make an early start for once.' She bustled off to wake the rest of the family up.

Spooker sighed. The trouble was, Sir Rupert's subject, Practical Haunting, was the most important one by far. After all, what good was a ghost who couldn't get out there and haunt? So Spooker was perfectly right to be worried. If he failed Practical Haunting, he'd have to repeat the year, and that would be just so humiliating. Everybody else in his family was so good at what they did …

Take his mother, for instance. She worked

part-time. She had a nice little job, moonlit nights only, pacing the corridors of Heversham Hall as the Lady in Blue. The Lady in Blue was thought to have been Lady Alice Ponsonby, who died of a broken heart in the sixteenth century because her father wouldn't let her marry the man of her dreams – a minstrel who had written a dreadfully soppy song about her, called, of course, *Lady in Blue*. Mrs Batt was supposed to have the strains of this song echoing after her as she paced, but she disliked it so much that she would only allow it on Hallowe'en and Midsummer's Eve. Spooker had been to watch her, and thought she was brilliant. Her weeping and wailing really were to die for, and the way she wrung her hands – well! He just hoped that one day he could be even half as heart-rending.

'Phanta, hurry up!' called Mrs Batt impatiently. 'Spooker's exams start today – we really mustn't be late.'

'I'm never late!' protested Phanta. *'He's* the one who's still in bed.'

Phanta was Spooker's little sister. Like many little sisters, she was a perfect delight to her parents and a perfect pain to her brother. She even kept her room tidy, which to Spooker seemed positively unnatural. Her parents called her Little Blossom, but as far as Spooker was concerned, she was the Evil Weed.

He gave up. He couldn't stay in bed and hide, much as he'd like to, so he trailed downstairs.

His father smiled at him. 'You look a bit green,' he said. 'Cheer up. How long do the exams go on for?'

'It's just Haunting History and Information Spectrology tonight. We've already had Dream-weaving and Poltergeist Studies. And then it's three nights for Practical Haunting.'

'There you are, then. It'll all be over inside a week. No problem. Now, time's getting on – is my cap straight?'

Mr Batt drove phantom trains. He'd started off driving a coach and horses – sometimes headless ones – along misty moorland roads. But he'd always hankered after steam, and now he drove ghost trains along lines that no longer existed. It was a very demanding job, but he loved it, and took pride in getting every detail right, down to his smart black uniform with its brass buttons and peaked cap.

'I suppose *you* must have been really good at exams, Dad,' said Spooker, wishing everybody wasn't in such a hurry.

'I don't think anybody likes exams,' said his father gently. 'The important thing is to stay calm. Don't panic, that's what you must remember.'

'Don't panic,' repeated Spooker, trying to get it into his head. 'Don't panic, don't panic …'

'Panic? Who's panicking?' demanded Mrs Batt. 'Mind you, I'll be panicking soon if you don't get a move on, Spooker. Have you got spare pens? And your exam timetable?'

'Oops.' Spooker realised he'd left it on his desk upstairs.

'I'm ready,' said the Weed.

She would be, thought Spooker. She did everything right, and she made sure the right people knew about it. No chance she'd ever muck up any of her exams. He went up to fetch his timetable, giving it a last anxious look before stuffing it into his bag.

'Come on, you two – get a move on! It's long

past time you were gone,' called Mrs Batt. ''Bye now. Have a nice night!'

What a joke, thought Spooker. With Practical Haunting first lesson, there was about as much chance of him having a nice night as there was of Sir Rupert turning up with a friendly smile, a kindly word, and a small good luck present for each of his students.

Chapter Two

All too soon, Spooker was in Sir Rupert's classroom, sitting over to one side in the hope that Sir Rupert wouldn't notice him there – he knew that teachers generally picked on people in either the front or the back row.

Sir Rupert swept in, wearing his usual velvet breeches, starched white ruff and with his sword at his side. He believed very strongly in tradition and was most comfortable in clanking chains and a suit of armour, because he felt that was the kind of thing people expected ghosts to wear. But armour and chains were too noisy for school, particularly as he liked to be able to creep up quietly and surprise unwary students – and staff, for that matter. He especially enjoyed taking his head off and leaving it on the desk to glare at the class, while the rest of him popped out to find someone else to annoy.

'Right,' he snarled, 'now as you know, you've got exams coming up. I'm expecting *extremely* good results – and what I expect, I usually *get* – isn't that right, Little Bo Peep?'

Little Bo Peep wasn't really called that at all. Her name was Holly, and she was very quiet and shy. Spooker thought that this must be why Sir Rupert often had a go at her – he didn't approve of gentleness.

'Yes,' she murmured, so nervous that she began to fade.

'Yes *what*?'

'Yes, Sir Rupert, sir.'

'Right. We're going to do some revision today, so there'll be absolutely no excuse for anyone to make a mess of things. Not even you,' he said, glaring at Spooker, who jumped nervously. 'Take notes. Revise all through the day before your practicals. Do whatever you have to do. But remember this: the In-spectres are going to be paying us a visit – and if any of you shows me up in front of *them*, you'll wish you'd never died!'

Spooker sighed. When things were bad, you could always be sure they'd get worse. As if it wasn't bad enough to have a psychotic teacher and exams coming up, now the In-spectres were coming as well.

The In-spectres had been introduced some years ago. The Powers-That-Be had decided that haunting standards were slipping. People just didn't seem to be scared of ghosts the way they used to be. Instead of screaming with terror and turning white overnight, they were just as likely to look extremely interested and whip out an infra-red camera. The Powers-That-Be decided it was all the fault of the schools, so they formed the Hit Squads and paid them lots of money to inspect the schools and make sure they were up to scratch. If there was one thing that was guaranteed to spook the spook teachers, it was the threat of a visitation from the In-spectre-ate.

Spooker's Aunt Jane was a teacher, and he'd once heard her explaining to his mother why teachers got so rattled about being inspected.

'It makes so much work, for one thing,' she'd said. 'You have to write down plans for every lesson, and you have to explain what your aim is, and set targets and things. And you have to be able to prove that you're good at getting your students through exams. Honestly, it's awful when they're in school – they can turn up in any lesson, they're just suddenly there at the back of the class with a clipboard, making notes on everything you say and do. It's enough to give you a nervous breakdown.'

'Still, dear,' his mother had said sweetly, 'at least you have those lovely long holidays to recover.' She hadn't sounded as if she had an awful lot of sympathy with the long-suffering teachers.

Spooker didn't either, but he had a nasty

suspicion that the In-spectres would make things even worse for the long-suffering students. If Sir Rupert was under pressure about exams, he would know exactly who to take it out on.

With a start, Spooker realised that everyone was looking at him. He turned round in a panic to see where Sir Rupert was. The teacher's voice boomed out behind him, like a cross between a foghorn and a bull with serious toothache.

'*When* you're ready, Spooker!'

Spooker whipped round, but too late. Sir Rupert was no longer there.

'*If* you don't mind …' Sir Rupert's voice was in his ear, a silky, scary whisper. '… then I'll begin!'

Spooker turned again. Sir Rupert's face was hanging a few inches in front of his own. His body was at the front of the room, ready to write on the blackboard. Spooker gulped. It paid to concentrate in Sir Rupert's class.

'Now then: Practical Haunting. Aims – that's what the In-spectres like, so that's what we'll give them. What are the aims of Practical Haunting? You there – Little Bo Peep.'

Holly trembled. 'Er – to – to remind people about things that happened in a place before,' she said nervously. 'Usually bad things, or sad things – like a murder, or—'

'Yes? Or what?'

'Er ...' Holly was floundering.

'Sir! Sir!' offered someone else. 'Someone who's died for love, sir!'

'Ye-es – love,' snarled Sir Rupert, looking as if he'd smelt something unpleasant. 'Yes, all right, all right, that can be part of it, but only a very small part. What are the other aims? Anybody?'

'To scare people, sir?' tried Spooker's friend, Goof.

'Now *that's* more like it! Yes, that's what we want to do; scare the— really frighten them a lot. Of course, it's fashionable these days to say that scaring people isn't the most important thing. *Some* people say you should try to do some *good* when you're haunting, try to make some kind of point.

'Well, let me tell *you*' – he broke off to glare round at them all, his eyes gleaming like hot coals – 'that as far as I'm concerned that's a load of new-fangled codswallop. I'm not interested in fancy theories. I want to see what you can do, not what you know. In short, what I want to see is people running out of well-haunted buildings, screaming their hearts out, with their hair standing on end. That's what'll get you the top grades, take it from me.

'Now, I want each of you to write down three Terrifying Techniques. Keep them simple, keep them practical. You've got two minutes.'

This was easy enough, thought Spooker. Planning how to scare people was all right – it was actually doing it that he didn't enjoy. He thought for a bit, and then wrote:

1. Put all the lights out.
2. Make the room freezing cold.
3. Transform into something really scary.

When their time was up Sir Rupert snapped, 'Spooker! Go on – amaze me! What've you got?'

Spooker read out what he'd put.

'Hm. Well, yes, that's all right, as far as it goes. Let's think about the apparition, then.

What can you make 'em see that'll really have them sucking their thumb and calling for Mummy?'

'Head under the arm!'

'Blood and gore!'

'Black monk's robe! Hood over the face!'

'Skulls with glowing coals for eyes!'

'Not bad,' said Sir Rupert approvingly. 'A bit predictable, but not bad. All right. Any questions?'

Spooker didn't mean to ask a question – he really didn't. It was never a good idea with Sir Rupert. But he couldn't help wondering, and then suddenly he heard himself speaking out loud:

'Sir, you don't think it's a bit cruel, do you, to make people so scared?'

The whole class gasped.

Sir Rupert stared at him. 'I don't believe I'm hearing this. Of course it's cruel! It's meant to be! You're a ghost, not a blooming pixie!'

Fortunately the bell went for break, so that Sir Rupert's attention was distracted.

'Remember,' he said, as everyone left the room. 'I'm the one who's doing the marking, so I'm the one you've got to please. You know how to do it. Don't let me down – think scary. If you don't, you'll be staying down a year, and then I'll have another chance to get it into your heads. That's all.' With a final glare at Spooker, he swept out.

Scary! Spooker groaned. The scariest effect he'd ever produced was a ghostly baby owl, cute and fluffy and quite horribly sweet. What was he going to do?

Chapter Three

In the staffroom a few minutes later, the headmaster, Chalky White, looked round at the teachers. Chalky was a kindly man who, after a hundred and fifty years of working with Sir Rupert, was wondering whether he should look into the possibility of early retirement. He wasn't sure how his staff were going to cope with a visit from the In-spectre-ate. He didn't feel very hopeful.

He waited patiently for Sir Rupert's head, which had been floating around the room annoying the other staff, to settle back on his body, and began to speak.

'As you know, the In-spectres are to pay us a visit. They may appear at any time. I have the greatest faith in every single one of you,' he said, crossing his fingers. 'I know you will give of your best, and I know just how good that best is.'

The Vanishing Lady, who taught Haunting History and was of a rather nervous disposition, quietly vanished.

'Eeeeeeeee!' shrieked the Irish Banshee, who

taught Games. 'Not the In-spectres, bejabers!'

'It's not that I mind anybody seeing what I do,' said Polly Geist carefully, 'but it's really *not* terribly convenient to have extra ghosts around when there are tables and dishes and things flying through the air. Ignorant people think it's easy, but it's not. It takes a lot of concentration to be a poltergeist, you know – a lot of skill.'

Sir Rupert snapped, 'What a lot of fuss! I don't see what the problem is – personally, I'm extremely confident.'

'Schemes of work all up to date?' enquired Chalky White mildly. 'Lesson plans all sorted? Records just as they should be?'

Sir Rupert snorted. 'Load of old cobblers. They'll know a top teacher when they see one.' But he had gone a little greener than usual. Paperwork was not something to which he generally paid a great deal of attention.

The only person who seemed perfectly calm was the teacher of Information Spectrology, Ged Goole. He was the newest member of staff, and by far the best organised.

'If there's anything I can do to help, Headmaster,' he said quietly, 'just say the word.'

'Thank you, Ged, thank you,' Chalky White murmured, watching the rest of his staff as each – in their own way – set about panicking. 'But I'm afraid it'll take more than Information

Spectrology to get us through this safe and sound ...'

* * *

'Come on,' said Goof, after Sir Rupert had left the room, 'let's go outside for a bit.'

'I'm going to stay in and look through my notes. I'm all right on the later stuff, but I can't remember much about Dark Age hauntings,' said Holly, fishing a book out of her bag.

'I don't think there's that much to remember, is there?' asked Spooker. 'It's mostly mounds, isn't it? Ghostly warriors marching out from ancient burial chambers, that kind of thing.'

'I can't remember,' she said. 'And it'd be just my luck if we got a question on it.'

'Yes,' said Spooker, worried. 'You've got a point there.'

'Oh, come on, Spooks, if we don't know it now, too bad. I want a break!'

So Goof and Spooker went out into the playground.

It was a beautiful night, and some of the younger students were playing Throughball in the brilliant silvery light of the moon. The Weed was on one of the teams. As Spooker watched, she made a feint to the left, and then whooshed round with an impressive turn of speed to send the ball in completely the opposite direction, so that it went straight

23

though an unwary member of the other side. The Weed punched the air with her hand and yelled 'Throughball! *Yes!*' and her team cheered and chortled.

'Look at her,' said Spooker gloomily. 'She's good at everything.'

'So are you. Well,' amended Goof, 'perhaps not everything. You're OK at Haunting History, aren't you? You're good at remembering things – much better than I am. And what about Dream-weaving? You got a merit for that last homework, the one to do with Scrooge.'

Ged Goole taught Dream-weaving as well as Information Spectrology. It wasn't one of the main subjects, unfortunately, but Spooker really enjoyed it. He'd been fascinated by the story Ged had told them of the haunting of Ebenezer Scrooge.

'It's about a miserly old man,' Mr Goole had said. 'One Christmas time, he has three dreams. The first reminds him of the Christmases he had when he was young and happy. The second shows him the kind of man he has become. And the third shows what awaits him in the future, if he doesn't do something about it. The experience is like a wake-up call for him – he's so horrified that he changes his ways completely. It's an interesting idea, isn't it?'

The homework had been to plan a similar series of dreams, this time for a bully instead of a miser. Mr Goole hadn't said how old the bully had to be, and Spooker had found himself thinking about Sir Rupert. It had been fun – though a bit of a challenge – to imagine Sir Rupert as a child, and to think about how he had to disguise him, of course, but that had been simple – he'd just turned him into a Maths teacher and given him a non-removable head, a shabby jacket with pens in the pocket, and a shirt and tie instead of a ruff and doublet.

'Yes, I enjoyed doing that,' he said. 'Much more interesting than skulls and chains and blood-curdling screeches.'

Just then, the Banshee gave her own very special version of a blood-curdling screech to mark the end of break.

Goof winced. 'Oh well,' he said, 'That's it, then. Time to go.'

* * *

The first exam was Haunting History, but even though it was one of his best subjects, Spooker still felt nervous as he sat down. The desks had all been moved as far apart as possible so that no one could cheat, and each had an exam paper laid face down on it. It made the room seem oddly unfamiliar, and even the Vanishing Lady looked anxious and fluttery. Anyone would think that she was doing the exam too, thought Spooker.

'You have an hour and a half,' she said gently. 'Remember to read the paper carefully – and if an In-spectre should appear – well, just try not to let it put you off.'

Spooker looked at the paper. None of the

words would go in; they seemed to be jumping about all over the page. He remembered his father saying, 'Don't panic.' He counted to ten, and had another go. This time the words settled down nicely and he was able to read quickly through the paper.

The first section was on sixteenth-century royal hauntings. He had to give three examples, explaining the reason for the haunting and describing it. This was excellent – he'd spent a lot of time revising this topic.

He began with Anne Boleyn, whose story had led to so many classic hauntings, and who was such an inspiration that his own school had been named after her.

Anne Boleyn was beheaded on 19 May 1536. Her death was ordered by her husband, King Henry VIII, who wanted to marry someone else.

One of the best known Anne Boleyn hauntings is at Blickling Hall in Norfolk. She spent a happy childhood here, but once a year, on the anniversary of her death, she appears in a coach pulled by headless horses, driven by a headless horseman, with her head resting in her lap.

---

* * *

For the second section, he had to choose an animal haunting and write about it. This was good – animal hauntings were his favourite. He thought about the phantom cat which haunts King John's Hunting Lodge in Somerset, but decided that it wasn't really interesting enough. All it did was walk through closed doors and curl up, go to sleep and disappear, so instead he wrote about the White Horse of Uffington.

He was just explaining how the horse, which is carved out of the turf on the side of a hill, comes to life once every hundred years and gallops over to Wayland's Smithy to have its hooves shod, when he suddenly had the feeling that he was being watched. He looked up.

A pair of glowing eyes was floating around the classroom. Other ghosts had noticed them too, and there was a little ripple of noise. The Vanishing Lady looked up.

'Oh! Is it – are you one of the—?' Then she began to look angry. 'Hang on a minute – I recognise those eyes! Sir Rupert, this is extremely unprofessional of you! You're disrupting my exam.'

'So sorry,' he cackled. 'Just dropped in to remind everybody of something.'

'Of what?' asked the Lady.

'That my eyes are upon you!'

And he howled with laughter as his eyes bounced from one student to another.

* * *

The final exam came after midnight. It was Information Spectrology with Mr Goole. They were in the computer room for this, so it didn't seem quite like an ordinary exam.

'Go into the folder named "Exam",' said Mr Goole. 'You'll see a picture of a castle. Have a look round it, and then open a document and write a design brief with your suggestions for three appropriate hauntings.

'Remember – a design brief has to be in three parts: Aims, Method, and Evaluation. That's the bit where you say how well you think you've done. Don't go on to the Spectrenet – you haven't got time. Anyway, I want *your* ideas, not somebody else's.'

The screen showed a model of a ruined castle. You clicked in each room, and up popped a little box with details of the things that had happened in it. There were portraits in some of the rooms, and you could click on those for more information about the people who'd lived there. It was just like playing a game to start off with, but Spooker soon realised there was a lot to do in one-and-a-half hours.

At the end, when they'd logged off, Mr Goole smiled at them.

'There, that wasn't too bad, was it? It looked to me as if you were coming up with some interesting new ideas – not too many hoary old heads-under-the-arms and clanking chains.'

'And what's wrong with clanking chains?' hissed Sir Rupert, appearing suddenly beside Mr Goole.

Mr Goole looked coolly at him. 'They're fine as long as they stay in the history books, but I think we ought to be able to manage something a bit more cutting edge in the twenty-first century – don't you, Sir Rupert?'

'Cutting edge? *Cutting edge*?' spluttered Sir Rupert. 'I'll give you cutting edge, you young—'

Chalky White appeared in between them. 'Is everything all right?' he asked politely. 'Only there's someone I'd like you to meet.'

A figure materialised beside him. It was a man wearing a black suit and holding a clipboard as if it were a deadly weapon. His eyes were colder than a blizzard in Alaska.

'May I introduce the Chief In-spectre?' said the headmaster.

Chapter Four

'And then Sir Rupert went all quiet,' chuckled Spooker just before bedtime, as he told his mother how the night had gone. 'It was really funny, Mum, only nobody dared to laugh because of the Chief In-spectre being there.'

'Sir Rupert was just the same when we were at school,' remembered Mrs Batt. 'I think the other teachers used to get quite cross with him. Mind you, some of them were a bit odd, too. Like the Banshee. I never could understand why they took her on to teach Games. All she was any good at was screeching.'

'To be fair,' said Mr Batt, who always was, 'Sir Rupert's good at what he does. He's just a bit old-fashioned. But at least he takes pride in his work.'

'Just as you do, dear,' said Mrs Batt fondly. 'No one's a better ghost-train driver than you are.'

'Will you just check my homework, Mummy?' trilled the Weed sweetly, obviously thinking it was about time she reminded everybody how wonderful she was. 'I've spent three hours on it, and it's not even due till next week.'

'Well done, dear. This looks terrific.' Mrs Batt smiled at her absently, and then turned back to Spooker. 'Are you sure you've got everything ready for going away?' she enquired anxiously.

For Practical Haunting, Spooker's class had to stay away from home. It was recognised that you needed at least three nights for a really good haunting; you had to build it up gradually. So the first night, maybe, you'd just lay on a mysterious drop in temperature. The second night, you'd add in another element – ghostly noises, perhaps, or mysterious lights. Then on the third night, you'd let loose with the grand finale, the full works – apparitions, furniture flying through the air, whatever was needed.

Mrs Batt was looking through his bag. 'I've packed you some spare clothes and your sleeping bag. I wonder if there's anything I've forgotten? I hate to think of you going off all by yourself – who knows where you'll end up? Or what kind of people you'll be with?'

'Now, now,' soothed Mr Batt, 'don't get the boy in a state. He'll be all right.'

'How do you know?' she demanded. 'Things have changed since we were at school – people don't have the respect for ghosts that they used to.

What if he comes up against someone who's seen that awful film – what was it called? *Ghostbusters*, that was it – you know, where they had ghost hunters with terrible weapons.'

Spooker stared at her. This wasn't helping at all.

'That was a story – pure fantasy. Don't take any notice, Spooks,' said Mr Batt hastily. 'Your mother's just anxious, because it's the first time you've been away by yourself. You'll have a great time, I'm sure you will. With a bit of luck you'll have a nice old mansion to haunt – creaky doors, echoing corridors, hidden rooms, the lot. I got the Tower of London for my last Practical Haunting exam – marvellous, it was.

There was just so much to choose from – headless queens, bloody traitors, guilty torturers ... Oh, it was such fun. I loved every minute.' He smiled, remembering.

But Spooker knew that Sir Rupert wouldn't make it as easy as that. The Tower of London was a dream assignment: the kind someone like Sir Rupert would only give to a favourite pupil, not to someone like Spooker.

'I suppose you're right,' said Mrs Batt. 'And anyway, the teachers will be round, keeping an eye on him.'

Was that supposed to cheer him up?

'I think I'll go up to bed and read through my notes again.'

His mother sniffed and looked determinedly cheerful. 'Oh no you won't. You'll go straight to sleep and get a good day's rest. Who knows how much sleep you'll get over the next few days?'

* * *

The day after his talk with Chalky White and the Chief In-spectre, Sir Rupert was also feeling a little anxious. He kept adjusting his head on his ruff, and swivelling it nervously from side to side.

'Now he knows what it feels like to be persecuted,' whispered Spooker to Goof.

'Your instructions are on the desks in front

of you,' Sir Rupert said. 'You've each been given a different location, and your – er – *aim* is to carry out the most effective haunting you can manage. What you're *really* after is to drive the inhabitants out – but it takes a lot of skill to do that, so I don't suppose any of you lot'll achieve it.'

A clipboard materialised. A pen marked a large cross.

Sir Rupert jumped. 'What I mean is, I have every confidence that you'll all do your very, very best. Remember, to avoid any possibility of cheating, you must stay on the spot. Myself or one of the other staff will be round at regular intervals to check up on you – to check that you're all right, I mean.' He tried to smile kindly at them. It was a horrible sight.

'Right – look at your instructions, and then whoosh off as soon as you're ready.'

Nervously, Spooker looked at the piece of paper. It said:

> Go to:
> 6 Buttercup Avenue
> Hookbridge
> Somerset.
>
> Your targets are the Roper Family:
> Cyril, Sandra and Ben

6 Buttercup Avenue? That didn't sound like a nice old mansion, where people would be expecting to see ghosts, so that half the work was done for you. It sounded new, and clean, and completely without cellars, ancient portraits or any atmosphere whatsoever.

If Spooker had had a heart, it would have sunk at this point. He glanced round. Everyone else had already gone, obviously eager to make a start. Sir Rupert was watching him. 'What are you waiting for? Go on! And, Spooker—' he said with an evil smile.

'Yes, sir?'

'Enjoy!'

Chapter Five

Soon, Spooker was hovering over Hookbridge. It was a small town, clustered round an old church. The streets in the centre were cobbled and most of the houses were hundreds of years old. He sensed that this was a place with lots of spectral activity – ghosts would be walking through doors, drifting up ancient staircases, re-enacting scenes from the past. Mostly, the people who lived in the houses would sleep comfortably, unaware of all the activity. Perhaps some would wake up and wonder about their dreams. One or two would welcome the ghosts, glad of the company.

Spooker was surprised. This wasn't what he'd expected. Maybe it wasn't going to be so bad after all. He began to feel a bit better. Perhaps Sir Rupert was softening up.

He whizzed round, looking at street names. High Street, The Lynch, Tweentown, Church Lane, Silver Street – but where was Buttercup Avenue? He whizzed up a bit higher to get a better view.

And then he saw it. A small, modern estate. A group of big detached houses that were so new that some of them were still being built. It was even worse than he'd expected. In fact, it was probably about as bad as it could be. Sir Rupert had given Spooker the almost impossible task of haunting a brand new house; a place that could have no history and no memories.

Spooker sighed, slid silently through a wall, and began to look round.

It seemed as if Mr Roper was in business. There was an office, with a computer, and shelves with box files. There were two desks in it; perhaps one was for Mrs Roper. Everything seemed to be very well organised.

Every room looked like a picture in a magazine. There were uplighters and downlighters, terracotta-coloured walls, artfully placed vases with nothing in them except a carefully arranged bunch of twigs, cunningly designed storage places, and absolutely no mess.

Except in one room. It was a bedroom, and it wasn't tidy at all. In fact it made Spooker feel slightly homesick, because it reminded him very much of his own room.

It looked as if the owner was someone who didn't know what cupboards were for, and who didn't believe in throwing things away. There were clothes all over the floor, and the shelves were crammed with books, dinosaurs made out of Lego, bits of wobbly pottery and piles of old exercise books. The owner of the room seemed to be interested in wizards: there were two large posters, and each had a wizard on it, along with several other strange-looking people. Spooker was rather disappointed to see that there were no pictures of ghosts, though. The tidiest bit of the room was the desk, which had a computer on it.

The room had a comfortable feel that the rest of the house did not, and Spooker caught himself thinking that he would definitely like the owner. He gave himself a little shake. Liking people wouldn't be much help when it came to haunting them. Think scary, he told himself sternly; in fact, think toe-curlingly terrifying. He had to plan. He had to manifest himself to the Ropers – he had to frighten them, whether he wanted to or not.

But where should he start? Usually when you went into a house, you got all sorts of vibrations – little shivers in time bringing messages from the past. That was how you found a starting place. But this house had nothing. It was cold and sterile. The only room where he felt even remotely comfortable was this one. There was a big squashy cushion in a corner, and Spooker lay down on it to wait for inspiration. But he'd had to get up early that evening, and he was tired. He'd just have a little rest, just close his eyes for a minute …

* * *

When he woke up, a boy was curled up in bed reading a book, and Mrs Roper had just come in.

'What's that you're reading, Ben?' she asked.

'Oh, nothing,' said Ben.

'Of course it's something. It's a book,' she said

sharply. 'Let me see.' She looked at the cover, and then turned it over to see what it said on the back. 'I can't understand why you like all this stuff about wizards and vampires and ghosts and werewolves. It's such rubbish. Why don't you read about real things, like football?' She handed it back in disgust.

'I don't like football,' said Ben.

'Well, I still think you could find something better than all those silly computer games you waste your time on. It's no wonder you're not getting on very well at school.' With that, she turned the light out and went downstairs.

Spooker felt sorry for Ben. It hadn't seemed a very affectionate way to say goodnight. He wondered if Ben had a teacher like Sir Rupert at school. Perhaps that was the real reason he wasn't getting on very well.

Thinking of Sir Rupert reminded him that he wasn't getting very far. He had to make a plan. Time was leaking away, and he only had three nights to make an impact. He knew he should try to look on it as a challenge, but somehow he just felt depressed. He sighed, and told himself to think positive.

He didn't know about Mr Roper, but Mrs Roper certainly didn't seem very sensitive. So whatever he did would have to be very obvious. And to please Sir Rupert, it would have to be very scary. Perhaps he should concentrate on what he was good at, which was animals. He needed a scary, obvious animal. He tried desperately to remember Sir Rupert's lessons about the use of animals in haunting ...

'Dogs – really the only choice for a classic haunting,' the teacher had said. 'Make 'em big, make 'em black, make 'em scary. And don't forget the glowing eyes. That's the bit that really freaks 'em.

'Oh, and the place for a phantom dog is on the moors – wild, deserted, and a nice bit of fog ...'

Well, Spooker couldn't do wild. The nearest thing to a moor was the Ropers' garden, which from what Spooker had seen of it, was a pocket handkerchief covered with gravel, wooden decking, and three spiky plants in pots.

Never mind – he'd manage somehow. There really wasn't any choice.

Chapter Six

It was dark now, and Ben was asleep. Spooker went downstairs to see what the elder Ropers were up to. They were in the sitting-room, talking.

'I do worry about Ben,' Mrs Roper was saying. 'He only got Cs on his last report. I think he should be working harder.'

'Yes, it's odd, isn't it?' said Mr Roper. 'He doesn't seem to have inherited our ability at all. I can't think what we're going to do with him. When I was his age I was already on my second theory of the origin of the universe, not messing about playing games and reading story books.'

'And I was developing a much more efficient way of solving simultaneous equations,' said Mrs Roper, trying to keep up.

'Children just aren't what they were,' sighed Mr Roper. 'Oh well, I must read this file before I go to bed. Honestly, some people think they can get away with anything. This chap owes us thousands of pounds – and he says he wants more time to pay, just because his business has folded.'

'I hope you're not going to give in.'

'You know me better than that, my love. He'll have to sell his house. In fact,' chuckled Mr Roper, 'he'll probably have to sell his children!'

Spooker was horrified. What an unpleasant man – and his wife seemed just as bad. He felt much better about doing a really nasty haunting now – in fact he was positively looking forward to it. The Ropers deserved all they were going to get.

He went back into Ben's room, where it was quiet and dark and felt friendly, and he thought hard.

He wanted to scare the older Ropers, but not Ben. With such awful parents and problems at school as well, Ben had quite enough to put up with already. At least Spooker only had the problems at school – oh, and the Evil Weed, of course. But irritating as she was, an annoying sister wasn't as bad as a double dose of deeply unpleasant parent. It shouldn't be too difficult to focus on Mr and Mrs Roper, he thought. Ben could quite easily be left out of it. He worked out what he had to do. Before long, he was ready to start.

First, he would build up the tension a bit: unexplained cold draughts; doors opening and shutting mysteriously; lights going on and off; all the usual kinds of things. Then, when the

Ropers were starting to get worried, he might try a Disembodied Voice. Black dogs usually foretold something nasty, so the voice could warn of something unpleasant that was about to happen. DVs were tricky, though; you had to be careful not to go over the top or they could just sound tacky.

The most difficult part would be manifesting as the fearsome dog. He thought he'd leave that till the next night, when he'd had a bit of a rest.

'Right,' he said to himself, 'time to get on with it.'

He went into the Ropers' bedroom and immediately set about task number one – THE BIG FREEZE!

Starting just under the ceiling in one corner of the room, Spooker whooshed very fast backwards and forwards. He kept on going back and forth, starting off a bit further down each time. When a ghost whooshes, it leaves a trail of cold air behind it. Spooker was weaving layer after layer of icy coldness.

The Ropers began to fidget and twitch. The further Spooker came down, the colder the room became. Soon, Mr Roper was trying to pull the duvet off Mrs Roper. Still half-asleep, she tugged it back again. The colder it got, the more determined each of them was to keep hold of the duvet. Soon, they were practically fighting each other. It was so funny to watch that Spooker got the giggles and could hardly keep whooshing. Finally they woke up properly.

'Cyril! Give me back the duvet! I'm freezing!'

'You're the one who keeps pinching it! Look, I'm shivering!'

'All right. That's your half, and this is my half.'

They pulled the duvet right up to their chins, but of course by now that didn't do them any good, because the room was colder than a polar bear's fridge.

'Cyril,' said Mrs Roper through chattering teeth, 'why is it so cold?'

Ah! thought Spooker. This is it. Any minute now she's going to realise there's something weird going on!

'Must be that cold front they mentioned on the weather. Mind you, I can't understand why it's so cold inside the house. I shall make a fuss about this, I can tell you – I didn't pay £200 000 for a house that can't keep the cold out. I'll be on the phone first thing tomorrow – I'm not putting up with this ...'

Mrs Roper sighed. 'I'm sure you won't, my love.' She got out of bed and plodded to the airing cupboard to fetch some blankets. Soon they were snoring again.

Spooker was disappointed. They'd been annoyed, but they hadn't been afraid, and it hadn't struck either of them that there was something unnatural – not to mention supernatural – about the sudden freeze. They really did seem to be dense. He was going to have to do something even more obvious. He decided to do some trickery with the lights.

It was very easy to divert a bit of spectral energy to interfere with the electrical circuits. Spooker soon had the lights in the bedroom flashing on and off, and the Ropers were soon awake again.

'Now what?' groaned Mrs Roper.

Mr Roper leapt out of bed and pressed the light switch. Nothing happened.

'This is outrageous!' fumed Mr Roper. 'There's

something wrong with the electrics too. Heads are going to roll for this—'

'Never mind that,' snapped Mrs Roper. 'What are you going to do about it *now*?'

'What's happening?' asked a sleepy voice.

Ben had been woken up by all the shouting. Spooker quickly switched the spectral energy off – he hadn't meant to disturb Ben.

Suddenly, a familiar voice snarled in Spooker's ear. 'What are you letting up for? Lost your nerve, have you?'

Spooker jumped. 'No, sir! Sorry, sir!'

'Well, see that you don't! Remember, an In-spectre could turn up anywhere – even in Buttercup Avenue – so don't think you're not being watched. I'm off now, but I'll be back.'

'Well, there's a treat in store,' muttered Spooker rebelliously, as Sir Rupert faded away.

He decided not to try the Disembodied Voice. The Ropers were making so much noise they probably wouldn't hear it anyway. It was getting late and he was tired – he'd used up a lot of spectral energy one way or another.

* * *

Ben was looking curiously at the spot where Spooker was.

'It's very cold in here, isn't it?' he said, still looking hard. 'Much colder than in my room.'

His parents took no notice of him. But that was

nothing new, and he wasn't thinking about it at the moment. He couldn't think about anything except the boy who was standing in his parents' bedroom. It would have been strange enough for any boy to be there, but there was much more to it than that. Because this wasn't a real boy. No real boy was pale and silvery like that. Even if he hadn't read all those ghost stories, he'd have known instantly that this boy was a ghost. A ghost in 6 Buttercup Avenue!

He went back into his own room, chuckling. This was *not* the kind of non-optional extra his parents had expected to have thrown in with their exclusive, executive, architect-designed home! This was brilliant!

Soon after, the ghost slid effortlessly through the wall and sat down on the floor cushion. This didn't seem to Ben the way that ghosts were supposed to behave.

'Aren't you going to disappear in a clap of thunder or something?' he asked.

The ghost leapt upright. 'What did you say?'

'I said—'

'No, I mean – can you see me?'

'Yes,' said Ben, 'of course I can. I wouldn't be talking to you otherwise, would I?'

'But you *shouldn't* be able to – oh, honestly, why do things always have to go wrong?'

Ben tried to cheer him up. 'I thought it was

funny, what you did in Mum and Dad's bedroom, with the cold and the lights. Are you going to do anything else?'

'Um, yes,' stammered Spooker. 'Well, that's the plan, anyway.'

'So you won't be going anywhere?'

'No. Not yet, anyway.'

'Good,' said Ben sleepily. 'Only it's nice, having somebody to talk to …'

Spooker felt wide awake. This was just like the fluffy owl incident – he'd made that when he was meant to be producing a giant vulture. People weren't supposed to like him; they were supposed to be afraid of him – at least if Sir Rupert was going to be happy. Not that he wanted Ben to be frightened – he liked him, and he felt sorry for him.

He sat thinking. Maybe, just maybe, he could do the right thing by everyone – help Ben out, perform a good haunting for the benefit of the Ropers, and get good marks from Sir Rupert. But it seemed a very tall order.

Chapter Seven

By the time dawn came, Spooker was asleep.

Huge black dogs with eyes like glowing coals loped through his dreams. They were chasing someone, hunting him down mercilessly. Spooker wondered who they were after. Then they opened their mouths – and Sir Rupert's voice growled, 'I'm going to get you, Spooker! You can't possibly escape!'

Then he realised that the dogs' eyes were Sir Rupert's eyes. They leapt towards him, but just as they were about to pounce, Phanta's clear little voice said, 'Down, boys! Leave him alone – after all, he is my brother!'

Spooker scrambled to his feet and turned to run for it – but there, in front of him, was a chorus line of eight-foot-tall In-spectres, complete with dark suits, glasses half-way down their noses, and clipboards. Glaring menacingly, they broke into a high-kicking song and dance act …

'*Your method is unsound.*
Your aims are quite unclear.

We don't think you should hang around,
You don't inspire fear!'

'I do, I do, I'm really scary!' cried Spooker, waking up in a panic.

'No, you're not,' said Ben kindly. He had been sitting at his computer, waiting patiently for Spooker to wake up. 'You're not scary at all.'

'But you don't understand – I've got to haunt your parents, that's the truth of it. I've got to frighten them, and I mean *really* frighten them, and I've got to do it in two more nights or I'll fail my exam.'

'What exam?' asked Ben, bewildered. 'I don't understand what you're talking about. I mean ghosts usually haunt a place because they died there, don't they? Not because they've got to do some exam!' He suddenly stopped. 'You – you didn't, did you?'

'Didn't what?'

'You know – die here.'

Spooker realised that Ben really didn't have a clue about ghosts. He began to explain. He told him about how you had to go to school to learn how to haunt professionally. He told him about the Anne Boleyn Secondary School, and about the Evil Weed and his troubles with Sir Rupert.

'The problem is,' he said, 'he's totally out of touch. He really is incredibly old-fashioned, not to mention nasty. But Practical Haunting is hugely important, and if I don't get good marks, I'll fail. I might even have to stay back a year. And I can't stand the thought of his face if that happens. Or the Weed's. Or my parents'. They'd be so disappointed.'

'Would they be cross?' asked Ben.

'Not cross. Just sad.'

'Mine get cross when I don't do well at school,' said Ben sadly. 'They think I'm stupid. When they think about me at all.'

Spooker didn't know what to say. He decided to change the subject.

'It's funny that you can see me. People are only supposed to see us when we want them to.'

Ben looked disappointed. 'Don't you want me to be able to see you?'

'Oh no, I didn't mean that! I'm glad you can, now. It's just that when I was – you know, doing that stuff in your parents' room – nobody was supposed to see me. I got it wrong. Perhaps I wasn't projecting a strong enough signal, or something.'

'I think it might be me,' said Ben thoughtfully. 'I think I've seen ghosts before. My gran lives in a house near an old ruined abbey, and I'm sure I've seen a ghostly monk there.'

'Is that right? Where would that be?'

'Marksbury Abbey. It's not far from here.'

'No kidding? Well, the monk you saw would have been my Uncle Albert. He's worked at Marksbury for years. He does a brilliant line in priests.'

'What are you good at?'

'I'm best at animal hauntings. In fact, that's what I've decided to do for the next stage in your parents' haunting. Last night was just a warm-up – well, more of a freeze-up really, I suppose. But tonight will be much more spectacular. Tonight, Ben, your mum and dad are going to see …' Spooker paused dramatically.

'What? What will they see?'

'Something so fearful it will haunt their dreams. Something so terrible it will cast a shadow over every waking hour. Something so—'

'Yes, yes,' said Ben, 'but *what*?'

'A fearsome spectral hound, huge and black, beyond your wildest imagining …'

'I can imagine big and black, no problem,' said Ben indignantly.

'… with eyes as red as the very fires of hell,' continued Spooker, ignoring him.

'I thought you said you couldn't do scary?'

'Oh, I'll be able to do this all right, no problem,' said Spooker airily.

Ben had heard people showing off before. 'Go on then,' he said. 'Do it!'

'Do what?' asked Spooker.

'Make the dog.'

'Make it?'

'Yes.'

'I don't exactly make it,' said Spooker.

'What do you do then?'

'Well – I turn into it.'

'Unreal! How?'

Spooker tried to think how to explain. 'It's to do with concentrating really, really hard,' he said finally. 'You have to gather every bit of spectral energy together, and you have to imagine what you want to turn into – sort of make a picture of it in your mind. And the other bit is that you have to focus on a feeling – the way the apparition will make the person who's being haunted feel. That's where I seem to go wrong,' he confessed. 'Sir Rupert says the feeling should be terror. But I don't think that's right. I think—'

Suddenly, he realised that time was getting on, and whatever he thought, he had an exam to pass.

'Well,' he said hastily, 'never mind all that for the moment, I'd better get on.' He looked anxiously at Ben. 'Are you sure you're OK with this? I mean, it could be – *should* be – pretty terrifying.'

'Don't worry about me,' said Ben happily,

'I'm looking forward to it.'

So Spooker concentrated, channelling all his spectral energy into visualising a monstrous black hound. But somehow, a different kind of dog kept poking its nose in.

* * *

Spooker opened his eyes and gave himself a little shake. Then he caught sight of his feet. They weren't black, they were golden. They looked much too big for his legs. He had an irresistible urge to roll over and slide on the floor and bounce.

Oh no! he thought. Scary spectral hounds don't play!

'Hey, Spooker! Is that really you? This is great – I've always wanted a dog. Mind you, it'd be nice if you were solid,' Ben said, as his hand went right through the dog's body. 'But you can't have everything. Come on – let's go outside.'

Part of Spooker knew that what he should be thinking about was haunting. But the biggest part just wanted to be a puppy.

They crept down the stairs, keeping as quiet as they could, and then they went into the back garden to play. They played chase and hide-and-seek behind the pots and the little shed, and it was more fun than Ben could ever remember having at 6 Buttercup Avenue.

They meant to be quiet, but Ben's feet made a noise in the gravel, and Spooker kept yapping, as puppies do. Neither of them saw the figure at the upstairs window.

Mr Roper was sleeping heavily. He was tired after last night's disturbed sleep. But Mrs Roper had woken up. She gazed at Ben as he romped about with a dog that she could only half see.

'Something strange is happening in this house,' she said to herself. 'I'm seeing things I don't usually see, and I'm feeling things I don't usually feel. I've never seen Ben playing like that before – and somehow, I think I should have done …'

The dog seemed to be teasing Ben. It

crouched, its tail wagging furiously. Ben circled round it, pretending to pounce. Then suddenly he did. The dog leapt out of the way – it seemed to be laughing – and Ben scrunched to a halt in the gravel.

The noise finally woke Mr Roper up. 'What's going on?' he said. 'Is there someone outside?'

'It's Ben,' said Mrs Roper.

'Ben? Outside? In the middle of the night?' He rushed over to the window.

'Who does that dog belong to? What does Ben think he's doing? Look what a mess he's making of the gravel!'

'He's playing, Cyril. He's having fun.'

'He's *what*? This is preposterous!'

'Do you know, I really like the look of it,' mused Mrs Roper.

But no one heard. Mr Roper had stomped off downstairs, to put a stop to it.

Chapter Eight

The next morning at breakfast Mr Roper was very grouchy.

'You've still not explained what you were playing at, Ben, messing about in the garden in the middle of the night. You'll have to rake that gravel at the weekend – I want it all neat and tidy again. And where did that dog come from? I've never seen one like that round here before.'

'What *was* it like?' asked Mrs Roper.

'It was – well, it was a sort of – a mixture, I think. I didn't manage to get a very good look at it. It just seemed to disappear when I went out into the garden.'

'Yes,' said Mrs Roper. 'It *did* just disappear. I was watching from upstairs. It was most odd.'

'I think it must have got under the gate,' said Ben. 'Anyway, I'd better clean my teeth. It's nearly time for school.'

He dashed upstairs and into his room.

'Psst! Spooker!'

Spooker was nearly asleep. It had been a very

tiring night and he needed his rest. 'Yes?' he said shortly.

'I think it's starting to work, with Mum anyway. I think she knows there's something funny going on.'

'Yes,' said Spooker. 'That's all very well. But it's not *supposed* to be funny. It's supposed to be *scary*.'

'Oh, yes. I was forgetting about your exam. Hey, it was good though, wasn't it? You were a great dog. See you later.'

Just after Ben had gone, someone else turned up. It was Mr Goole.

'Hello, Spooker. Well, this is all very interesting, isn't it?'

'Interesting?'

'Yes. You're certainly beginning to have an effect on the Ropers. Even if it wasn't quite the one you intended.'

'Do you think so?' Spooker was confused. 'Neither of them seems a bit scared.'

'Hauntings don't have to be scary, Spooker. You know that.'

'Sir Rupert seems to think they do,' said Spooker gloomily. 'In fact, according to him, the whole point of the task is to frighten the Ropers so much that I actually drive them out.'

'That isn't what it says on your instructions. Do you remember? You're supposed to "carry out the most effective haunting you can manage." Concentrate on that. Think about what you really want to do in this house. Things are starting to change – and that's because of you. Ben's been happier since you came, hasn't he? Remember – haunting doesn't have to be just about giving people a fright – it can be about making people look at things in a new way. You've started something, Spooker, even if you didn't mean to. All you have to do now is finish it.'

* * *

Spooker thought about what Mr Goole had said. He didn't understand all of it, but he thought it was true about Ben. It didn't seem as if he usually had much fun. As far as Spooker could see, the Ropers didn't want their well-organised life disturbed by a messy, noisy child, and so Ben had learnt to keep out of the way. He didn't seem to have other children round to play much – probably because the Ropers thought they'd make even more mess – so he spent most of his time alone in his room. Spooker couldn't imagine the Ropers having fun with Ben. In fact he couldn't imagine them having fun at all.

But he couldn't really see what any of this had to do with his Practical Haunting exam. Whatever Mr Goole thought about the future of haunting, the present of haunting was that it was Sir Rupert who would give him his marks,

64

and Sir Rupert would most certainly not be impressed by what he'd done so far.

Which only left tonight. He had to do something which would make both the Ropers realise, without a shadow of a doubt, that they were being haunted. From what Ben had just said, it sounded as if Mrs Roper was beginning to get the message. That was all very well, but there was still a long way to go. He mustn't go to sleep till he had a plan. He really musn't – but he did feel so tired …

*   *   *

It was already dark when he woke up. Ben wasn't in his room, so Spooker could concentrate.

'Right,' he said to himself. 'Think! What am I going to do? It's got to be something really obvious, or Mr Roper won't even notice …'

He tried to remember what they'd done in school. Sir Rupert had mostly taught them traditional ghosting techniques, based on historical hauntings – but since Buttercup Avenue had no history to speak of, they were no use to him. Then he thought about Poltergeist Studies. Perhaps that was the answer – a bit of poltergeist activity? Surely flying plates and moving furniture would be obvious enough? The only snag was that he'd never paid much attention in Miss Geist's lessons. There was a lot of potential for messing about in Poltergeist Studies, and Miss Geist didn't have Sir Rupert's knack for ensuring obedience.

Something was happening. Spooker noticed that the room was getting lighter. There was an unearthly glow coming from one corner.

Ah, thought Spooker, more visitors.

A massive black dog, bigger by far than any mortal species, appeared in the midst of the phosphorescent glow. Its eyes were terrible, red and glaring, and blood dripped from its savage mouth.

'Is that you, Sir Rupert?' enquired Spooker politely.

Sir Rupert looked round the untidy room in distaste.

'I've been keeping an eye on you, Spooker,' he snarled, 'and I'm not very happy with what I see. You're not here to make friends and influence people, no matter what Goole might have been telling you. You're here to make them very – and I really do mean *very* – frightened. Nice little puppy dogs aren't going to do that, are they? Look at me, Spooker Batt. Look and learn. You've got one night left. Make it count.'

He began to swell in size, but unfortunately, the room was too small to hold him comfortably.

'Oh dear, sir,' said Spooker, 'that's the trouble with these new houses. Here, let me help – perhaps if you bend your head down, and curl your tail in – no? Oh well then – be seeing you, sir …'

With a menacing snarl, Sir Rupert faded swiftly away. Spooker wondered if the In-spectres were to blame for all this attention. Perhaps the teachers were all queuing up to get out of their way, and that was why he didn't seem able to have a minute's peace.

As Spooker's grin faded, he suddenly realised

what his real problem was. It wasn't that he *couldn't* do it – he didn't even *want* to do it. It was all very well to talk about terrifying people when you'd never met them and didn't care about them. But Spooker definitely didn't want to frighten Ben, and although he didn't much like them, he didn't really want to terrify Ben's parents either. But he had to try, or he'd fail. It was as simple as that.

Ben came in. 'Oh, hi Spooker – you're awake! What are we doing tonight? Is it the scary dog again?'

'No. That didn't work, did it?'

'Well, they did see it. And it's done something to Mum. She keeps smiling, and she asked if I wanted to play any games after tea. I didn't really, but she looked so keen that I said I would – and do you know, we had quite a laugh. Dad looked a bit puzzled. He asked her if she was sickening for something.'

'Oh!' Spooker pondered. So Mr Goole had been right. Things were changing. Change … that reminded him of something. What was it?

And then he had it. It was the story of Scrooge.

'So what's it going to be?'

'Just a minute, I'm thinking,' said Spooker. 'You enjoyed last night, because it was fun, didn't you?'

'Yes,' said Ben, looking puzzled.

'And your mum's started laughing and acting like she wants to have fun as well.'

'Yes, I suppose so.'

'So if your dad learnt how to have fun too, then things would really change around here?'

'Yes, but you'll never change Dad!'

Spooker had it. He knew what he was going to do. He smiled.

'Don't you be so sure,' he said. 'Stranger things have happened ...'

Chapter Nine

Meanwhile, Mrs Roper was sleeping soundly. But Mr Roper was not so lucky.

He was so restless that in the end, he got up and went into the spare room, so that he wouldn't disturb his wife. But as soon as he went back to sleep, the dreams began again. He couldn't seem to lie still, and he kept muttering things.

'What's going on, Spooker?' asked Ben. They were crouching in a corner of the room.

'I'm dream-weaving. Shush, I've got to concentrate, or he'll stop.'

After a while, Mr Roper grew calmer. Ben thought he could hear sounds, and see dim pictures – a bit like when you look at the beam from a film projector. He squinted – there was a child – and wasn't that Ben himself? And his mother? The pictures were moving too fast for him to be able to see properly; there seemed to be lots of separate images, flowing around the room and then weaving together into a sort of ribbon which wound itself round his father's bed, until eventually, Mr Roper woke up. He got out of bed, not noticing Ben or Spooker, and went quietly downstairs. He went into his study and turned on the computer.

Ben couldn't go into the room, because the lights were on and his father would have seen him. So he couldn't see what Mr Roper was doing, and Spooker wouldn't tell him.

'You'll see in the morning,' he said, looking pleased with himself.

Mr Roper spent an hour on the computer and then went back upstairs. Soon he was fast asleep – and this time, there were no dreams to disturb him.

'Now, I've just got to do a bit of poltergeisting in your mum's room, and then you can show me some more of your computer games.'

Spooker wouldn't let Ben watch him as he worked – he wanted it all to be a surprise. So Ben had no idea what he was up to. He didn't hear any bangs or crashes, so he assumed Spooker hadn't been throwing furniture about or breaking pots, which was what he thought poltergeists usually did.

They played games till Ben was too tired to play any more. When he'd shut the computer down, he said suddenly, 'You said you had three nights for the haunting, didn't you?'

'Yes,' said Spooker. 'That's right.'

'So … this is the last night. You won't go before I wake up, will you?'

'No, of course I won't. I want to see what happens tomorrow. And even when I do go, I won't be far away – I'll come back and see you, don't worry about that.'

'Good,' said Ben firmly. 'It's been nice having someone to play with. Mum and Dad don't like me having people round. They say they work hard and they want peace and quiet when they're at home, not noise and mess.'

'I think,' said Spooker, 'that might change. With a bit of luck,' he added, crossing his fingers.

A squeal of astonishment woke everyone up the next morning. Ben rushed into his mother's room.

'Look, Ben, look!' she whispered.

The room was filled with flowers – lilies, tulips, roses, cornflowers and delphiniums. Bunches of blue and silver balloons with streamers of gold ribbon bobbed about near the ceiling.

Mr Roper came in, looking sleepy and puzzled.

'Cyril! Did you do this?'

He stared at the flowers. 'They're beautiful, aren't they?'

'But you never give me flowers! You've

always said they're a waste of money! And how did they get here in the middle of the night?'

'I – I don't know. But – there's more.'

'What? More flowers?'

'No. No – I had these dreams, you see. About when I was a child, and my father wouldn't let me play with the other children because he wanted me to study. After a bit, they stopped asking, and then I pretended I didn't like playing anyway, and before long I even believed it. And then there was another dream, an awful dream. Ben was ill – desperately ill. You are all right, Ben, aren't you? It was a dream, wasn't it?'

'Yes,' said Ben, bewildered, 'I'm fine.'

'Thank goodness! I was so afraid – and then

there was another dream.' He turned to Mrs Roper. 'You were going away, and I was all alone.'

He wiped a tear from his eye. Spooker, who was watching, began to think he'd overdone it a bit. This was getting embarrassing.

'And then I woke up and I realised it wasn't too late, so I went downstairs and ordered some things over the Internet.'

'You did what?' asked Mrs Roper, looking thoroughly confused.

'I don't exactly know what I ordered – it all seemed a good idea at the time, and that's all I can really remember ...'

'I'll go and see,' said Ben, who dashed downstairs, switched on the computer and found several e-mails confirming orders that his father had made during the night. He also checked the outbox and printed off the e-mails his father had sent. He read through them carefully, and then read through them again in case he'd made a mistake. Then he tore back upstairs.

'Look!' he said. 'You've booked a camping holiday to France, and you've ordered three mountain bikes! And you've sent an e-mail to someone who owes a lot of money, saying he can have more time to pay, and you've given lots of money to Children In Need, and there was a big note to yourself stuck on front of the computer saying, "ORGANISE HOUSE-WARMING PARTY!"'

Mr Roper fainted, and Mrs Roper fanned him tenderly with a bunch of balloons.

It was time for Spooker to go. He knew Sir Rupert wouldn't be happy with what he'd done, to put it mildly. Ben was, though, so that was something. He just hoped it would last, and that the Ropers wouldn't slip back into their old ways.

'You made all that happen, didn't you?' demanded Ben. 'It's brilliant! I've never seen them like this. But what happened to being scary?'

'Don't worry about it,' said Spooker grandly. 'That's my problem. But now I have to go, or I really will be in trouble.'

'All right – but don't forget, you said you'd come back!'

And as he watched, Spooker seemed to slip through an invisible door, and then he was gone.

* * *

'And so I think it went very well, even if Sir Rupert doesn't see it that way,' Spooker finished. He had been explaining to his parents about what had happened.

'Well, I think it sounds wonderful,' said his

mother, loyally. 'I love the bit about the flowers and the balloons. Mrs Roper must have been thrilled.'

'And manufacturing dreams – that's very advanced stuff. I think you've done brilliantly,' said his father.

'Anyway,' said Mrs Batt, 'Off to bed now. Have a good sleep, and then you'll be ready to face Sir Rupert tonight. And remember – we're proud of you, whatever he says.'

Chapter Ten

Everyone was full of their adventures when Spooker got into school that night. Goof had had a Tudor mansion, which had once been the home of a poet called Sir Walter Wessex, who had been in love with Elizabeth I and written her some quite astoundingly awful poems. She had got so fed up of him spouting forth at every verse-end that she had sent him packing back to his mansion, where he spent the rest of his life – and death – trailing up and down the corridors reciting poetry.

Goof had thoroughly enjoyed himself. 'The best bit was when a Women's Institute bus trip came round the house. I managed a daytime haunt. I had a copy of Wessex's *Collected Poems*, so I recited them to the ladies, looking all soulful and pathetic, and they lapped it up! They all rushed off to the shop to buy their own copies.'

Holly had had a badly overgrown garden. 'It was so sad. There was this old lady living in the house the garden belonged to, but she couldn't get out into the garden any more – she was stuck inside because she was in a wheelchair. So I fixed it so that whenever she looked out of the window, she saw the garden as it used to be. She was thrilled. I didn't scare anybody, but I don't care.'

'So none of us really scared anybody,' said Spooker. 'I certainly didn't.'

He was just beginning to tell them about 6 Buttercup Avenue when the Banshee screeched the beginning of lessons, and it was time for Practical Haunting.

'I expect you'll all be wanting to know your

marks,' said Sir Rupert, smiling (nastily of course – he never smiled any other way). 'Well, tough luck. Teachers are busy people. You'll have to wait. However, I did of course visit you all while you were in action. So I do have some preliminary remarks to make.

'You know, when you're a teacher, you always hope that one day you're going to come across a student who's really and truly brilliant. Generally – you don't. You're much more likely to come across people who are completely and utterly useless.

'But you don't often have the privilege of

teaching a whole *class* of students who appear to have sat through a whole year of your incredibly wonderful teaching and taken in precisely nothing. This year, however, I—'

A small ghost appeared. Trembling, she said, 'Please, sir …'

An expression of disbelief crossed his face. 'Are you *interrupting* me?'

'Please sir, sorry sir, but …'

'Do you *know* who you're talking to?'

She seemed to have lost the power of speech.

Sir Rupert bent down, and said very quietly, 'Go away. *Now.* Or—'

But before he could go on, the headmaster himself appeared.

'Is there a problem? I sent the child to tell you that the Chief In-spectre has called a special meeting of the whole school in the hall.'

'But I'm in the middle of—'

'I'm well aware of what you are in the middle of, Sir Rupert. But the In-spectres are ready for us. Shall we go?'

Scowling horribly, Sir Rupert marched his group into the hall.

The In-spectres were sitting in a row on the stage. Chalky White went up to sit with them, and the Chief In-spectre stood up to speak.

'We are coming to the end of our time here,' he said. 'And although our full report will not be completed for some weeks, we have decided to give you a summary of our findings.'

He stopped, and frowned over his glasses at the assembled staff and students.

'Most of the teaching at the Anne Boleyn Secondary School is sound. Some of it is outstanding. And some of it' – he paused. It seemed as if he was having trouble finding the right words – 'is absolutely abysmal.'

The teachers were by now looking completely confused, except Sir Rupert who was smirking.

'I have already discussed these findings in more detail, of course, with your headmaster.

'As part of deciding how good teachers are at teaching, we have to look at how much their students have learnt. With this in mind, we have kept a very close eye on those students who have been doing their Practical Haunting. This gave us an ideal opportunity to see just how much use their education has been to them so far.'

Sir Rupert began to look less confident. He glared at Spooker, who had been watching him with interest, and scowled at the others.

'We observed all of the students at intervals during their practicals. And we have been' – he paused, and looked round the room – '*incredibly* impressed by what we have seen. The students of this school took a flexible and creative approach to the tasks they were given, even when those tasks were *unreasonably* difficult.' The glance he gave Sir Rupert had icicles in it. 'They can truly be said – sometimes *in spite* of their teachers – to be forging ahead with the task of taking ghosting into the new millennium.'

'What's he on about?' whispered Goof to Spooker.

'Don't know,' whispered Spooker, 'but I think we're OK.'

'In particular – and this is a very unusual step – I wish to single out one particular student for the most effective and life-changing piece of haunting we have ever seen in students of this level.

'Spooker Batt, please come forward!'

'What?' said Spooker.

'Who?' asked Sir Rupert.

'Well done!' smiled Ged Goole.

'He's my brother, you know,' boasted Phanta.

* * *

After the In-spectres had gone, Chalky White decided to throw a party for staff, students and parents. Music was by the Banshee, who in her spare time was a singer in a rock band, Banshee and the Wailers. They were pretty lethal, so everyone was relieved when Chalky asked for quiet.

'This has been an eventful week for all of us at the Anne Boleyn Secondary School, and I want to thank all of you for your support and hard work.

'You may have noticed that Sir Rupert Grimsdyke is not with us tonight. Sir Rupert has served the school loyally for many, many years. But he has now decided that the time has come for him to move on. He has decided to move to Hollywood, where he feels he has a future in the special effects industry. Until we are able to appoint a new member of staff, his duties will be shared by the other teachers.

Now – let the party continue!'

For a moment, there was a stunned silence from all the students. Then Spooker, with a huge smile on his face, said it for all of them.

'Un*real*!'

Look out for more

fantastic fiction in

Black Cats ...

TERRY DEARY
Footsteps in the Fog

Laura Lund's family is rich.
Tommy Pickford's family is poor,
but he and Laura are best friends
and look out for each other all the time.

Their school, Meek Street Primary,
is having a special mid-winter treat:
a show starring the famous magician,
The Great Marvello.

But Marvello's tricks seem too good
to be true, and soon Tommy and
Laura are plunged into danger …

PHILIP WOODERSON
Moonmallow Smoothie

Sam's dad runs an ice cream parlour,
but his business is fast melting
away, thanks to competition from
Karbunkle's Mega Emporiums.

Then, suddenly one night,
a meteorite crashes to Earth in Sam's
garden. It's not just space-rock –
its special properties are perfect for
making ice cream. Soon everyone
wants a taste of Dad's latest invention,
called Moonmallow Smoothie.

But Sam's troubles are only
just beginning …

LYNDA WATERHOUSE
Drucilla and the Cracked Pot

Drucilla is famous for causing trouble –
but she isn't always to blame …

She didn't sell Pontius Maximus –
the Roman Army officer – a broken
pot, and it wasn't *her* toy chariot he
slipped on. It wasn't *her* idea for Mum
to get re-married and go back to Rome
to live. And as for finding the curse …

How does Drucilla cope with the
chaos and confusion of her life?

KAREN WALLACE
Something Slimy on Primrose Drive

When Pearl Wolfbane and her family
move into No. 34 Primrose Drive,
everything soon becomes murky, weird
and crumbling. Except for Pearl's room.
It stays pink, frilly and normal because
Pearl isn't like the rest of her family.

When Pearl meets her neighbours,
the Rigid-Smythes, she is delighted.
They have a swimming pool, not a
swamp; a kitchen, not a dungeon.

But they also have a daughter
called Ruby, and she isn't like her
family either …

Other titles available in Black Cats …

Great stories for hungry readers